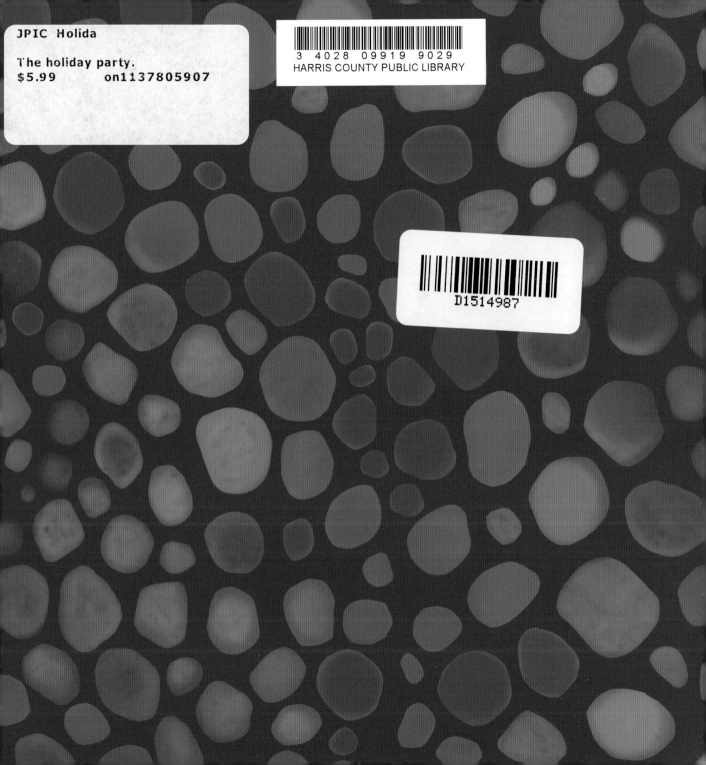

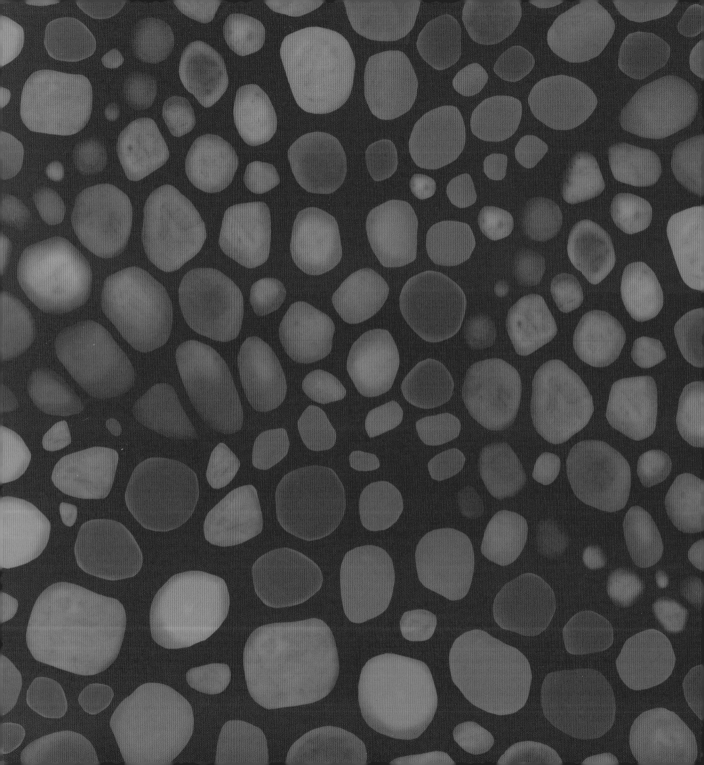

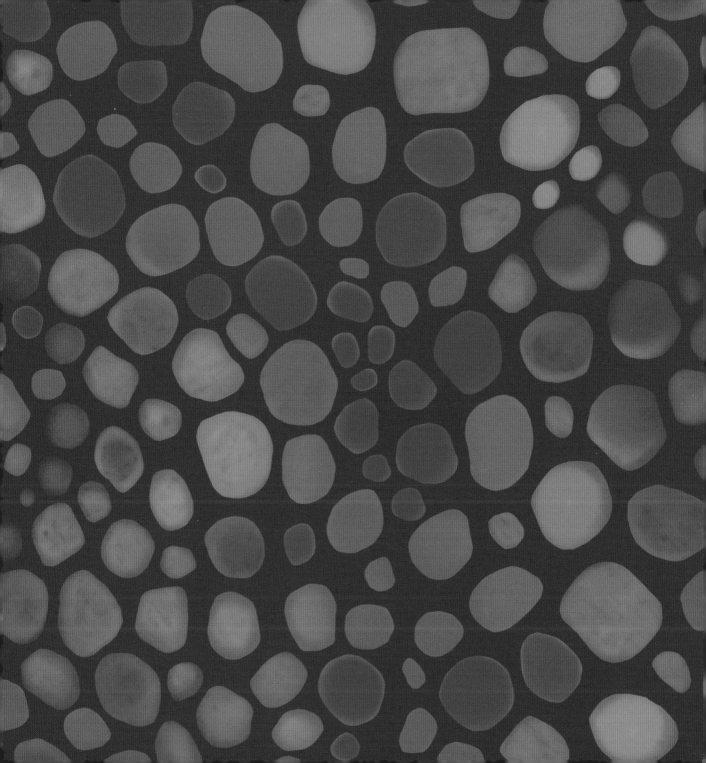

First US edition 2020
First published by Templar Books, an imprint of Bonnier Books UK, 2020

Library of Congress Catalog Card Number pending
ISBN 978-1-5362-1340-9

20 21 22 23 24 25 TLF 10 9 8 7 6 5 4 3 2 1

Printed in Dongguan, Guangdong, China

This book was typeset in Kosmik BoldOne and Kosmik PlainTwo.
The illustrations were created digitally.

Candlewick Entertainment
an imprint of
Candlewick Press
99 Dover Street
Somerville, Massachusetts 02144

www.candlewick.com

GIGANTOSAURUS™

THE HOLIDAY PARTY

CANDLEWICK
ENTERTAINMENT

It was early morning in Cretacea. Tiny stretched out her arms and smiled at the sunrise. The little dinosaur hurried to find her friends. She wondered what exciting things they would do today.

"I can't wait to get started!"

It's going to be another SUN-SATIONAL day!

But Bill, Mazu, and Rocky weren't excited in the slightest.

"Isn't today the SHORTEST day of the year?" yawned Bill.

"Yes," grumbled Mazu. "It's the day the sun rises the latest and sets the earliest."

Rocky gave his ball a grumpy kick. There wasn't enough time to have any fun.

Tiny caught the ball on her head, but her friends didn't even smile.

"What if I found a way to make the shortest day just as fun as every other day?" she suggested.

Mazu wasn't sure. "How can it be fun when it's shorter?"

We can have a holiday party! And keep it going after sunset!

"But you'd need lights," sighed Mazu.

"And food," chipped in Bill. "LOTS of food."

"Yes!" said Tiny. "All kinds of stuff! I'll invite everybody!"

It was settled. Tiny was having a holiday party! The delighted triceratops skipped around Cretacea, giving out invitations to everyone she saw.

Along the way, she sang a little song.

Please come to my party, my holiday party. You'll see that this day is the funnest of fun!

Tiny sang on and on. She described yummy food, music, games, and magical decorations—plus presents for everyone!

Please come to my party,
my holiday party.
I'll show you this day
is the BEST of the year.

Tiny's friends gathered around. At first they were annoyed at being disturbed, but the plans sounded so SPECTACULAR, they started to get excited. Everyone agreed to come!

STOMP! STOMP! STOMP! The ground shook . . . and GIGANTO appeared!

Tiny gulped nervously, then stepped forward so the huge dinosaur could see her.

W-w-would YOU like to come to my party?

"ROOOARRR!" Giganto said, then disappeared back into the jungle.

"I'll mark you down as a 'maybe'!" Tiny said.

Tiny worked hard all day preparing for the holiday party. She'd decided to have it up in the Frozen Lands, so she packed everything onto her sleigh, and Bill, Mazu, and Rocky hitched a ride through the snow.

Tiny whooshed across the ice, pulling her friends behind her. At last the sleigh skidded to a stop in front of a big green tree.

BUMP! Everything Tiny had brought tumbled onto the snow—there were boxes and packages everywhere.

"Too late!" shouted Mazu. "Look!"

Tiny gazed across the snowy mountains. Her guests were nearly here!

"Oh no," she gasped. "I spent so long telling everyone about the party, I didn't leave any time to set it up!"

She didn't know what to do.

Tiny's friends couldn't wait for the fun to begin.

"Welcome to my holiday party!" said Tiny, unpacking everything in a hurry.

The little dino did her best, but nothing went the way she had planned.

Where are those games you promised?

And the glorious decorations!

"Oh, right," stammered Tiny, grabbing some garlands. "Decorations!"

She tossed the garlands up onto the tree, but they tangled messily in the branches.

"Umm . . . interesting choice . . ." said Archie.

"Where's all the food?" demanded Rugo the rugosodon.

"Right here, as promised," said Tiny. "Have some fruit!"

Rugo swallowed the berry in one gulp, then shrieked in surprise. It was ice-cold!

Tiny shrugged uneasily. "I guess that's why they call it the Frozen Lands."

BRAIN FREEZE!

"And where are the tunes?" said Ignatius. "You said there would be music."

"I've got lots of instruments in here," replied Tiny. She threw a huge trumpet over to him, but Ignatius could barely hold it, let alone play!

The poor dino fell backward into the snow.

Tiny's holiday party was turning into a DISASTER. Totor and Cror decided to go home.

"Boring games, frozen food, and bad music," snapped Totor.

Do you call this fun?

We call this DULL!

More guests began to grumble. One by one, they trudged away.

"Don't leave!" begged Tiny. "We're only getting started! I have presents for everyone!"

She staggered across the snow carrying an ENORMOUS pile of gifts wrapped in bright colors.

But the pile began to wobble, and Tiny stumbled in the snow. OH NO! The parcels tumbled down the frozen mountain, falling into a deep hole at the bottom.

Rocky, Bill, and Mazu ran to their friend.

"Tiny!" gasped Rocky. "Are you all right?"

Tiny burst into tears. All she wanted was to show everyone that even the shortest day of the year could be the best!

"Maybe you're right," she sobbed. "Maybe today is just NO FUN at all."

Tiny's friends knew how hard she was trying. But before they could help her,
a terrible roar shook the mountains. One more guest was on his way . . .

GIGANTOSAURUS!

The other dinosaurs were furious.

"What's HE doing here?" they demanded.

"I invited him . . ." Tiny said. "He deserves to have fun, too."

Tiny stepped out to greet the big, scary dinosaur.

"I'm sorry I invited you out here," she said sadly. "I know I promised you lots of food and presents."

Giganto glared down at the frightened party guests. Then he thumped his tail hard against the ice. The ground began to shake.

BOOM! BOOM! BOOM!

Tiny and her friends found themselves being bounced up and down.

Giganto was trying to PLAY with them! Dinosaurs went sliding around in circles and icicles jingled merrily in the tree.

Tiny was confused. The party was in full swing even without food, decorations, or presents.

"All those things you came for," she said. "They never happened!"

But Tiny's friends hadn't come for the promises . . .

That's when Tiny knew that her holiday party was going to be OK after all.

"Thanks, you guys. It's not the treats that make a party, it's the friends!" she cried. "Right, Giganto?"

Giganto replied with another careful tail thud, lifting the decorations on the tree and undoing all the tangles.

Now the tree was perfect.

But Giganto wasn't quite finished. He hit the ground again, even harder, shaking the mountain so hard the lost presents bounced up out of the hole.

"Thank you, Giganto!" gasped Tiny, running to collect them.

What a party it turned out to be. When night fell, Cretacea turned into a winter wonderland!

Tiny took out a gigantic walnut, carefully wrapped in leaves, and presented it to Giganto.

"This is for you," she said with a smile. "Happy shortest day!"

ROAARRR! Giganto had enjoyed the holiday party, too!

Everyone cheered. "BEST DAY EVER!"

"Thanks, guys," said Tiny. "We should celebrate like this every year!"

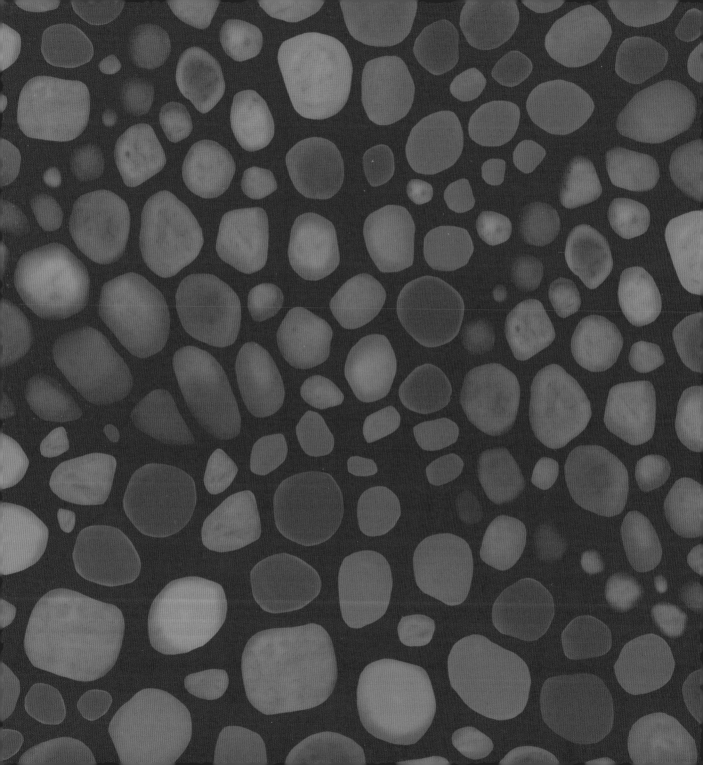

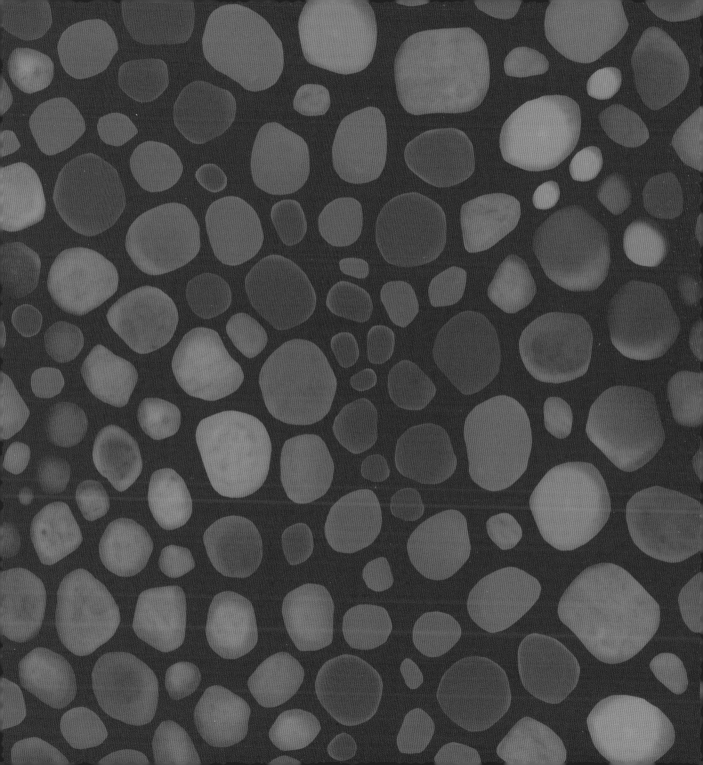

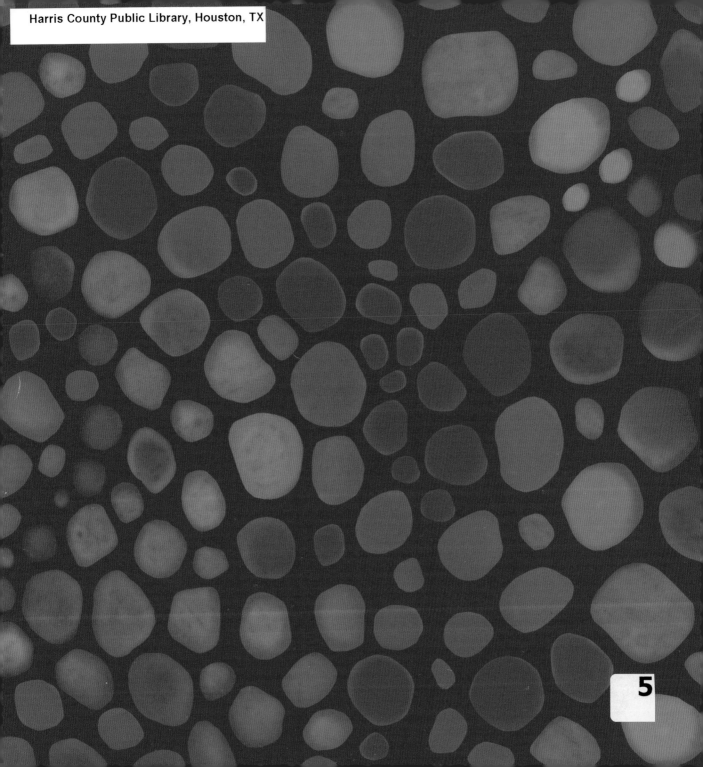

5